Ballerina Stories

igloo

Contents

The Best Ballerina. . . . page 6

New Slippers for Daisy. . . . page 14

Davina, Prima Ballerina. . . . page 22

The Reluctant Ballerina. . . . page 30

Ballet School in Trouble. . . . page 38

Old School, New School. . . . page 46

The Magic Music Box. . . . page 54

Anna's Audition. . . . page 62

Rosie's Wish. . . . page 70

Lily the Ballet Star. . . . page 78

Stage Fright. . . . page 86

Ruby Saves the Show. . . . page 94

Clumsy Clara. . . . page 102

The Ordinary Tutu. . . . page 110

Lisa in the Limelight . . . . page 120

May the Best Team Win. . . . page 128

Goodbye, Miss Sweet. . . . page 136

Flowers for Princess Prunella. . . . page 144

Boys Don't Dance. . . . page 152

The Best Ballerina

It was almost time for ballet class at Miss Fontaine's School of Dance. Girls dressed in different-colored tutus stretched their arms and pointed their toes. On a bench, at the back of the room, Sophie sat, putting on her ballet shoes. She hadn't been coming to the class very long and she felt a bit shy.

Suddenly, Angelica Brown burst in and went straight over to the mirror. Angelica was the best ballerina in the class and she knew it. She was confident, popular and a bit bossy.

6

Angelica's friend, Rose, had been warming up in front of the mirror. Angelica pushed her out of the way. "You're doing it all wrong, Rose," she said. "Look, I'll show you how to do it properly." Angelica balanced her foot on the barre and bent forward, gracefully.

Just then, Miss Fontaine appeared with a small, blond girl. "Listen, everyone," Miss Fontaine called, clapping her hands. "I want you to welcome Lottie to our class."

Angelica immediately marched over and took Lottie's hand. "Come and stand next to me," she said. "I'll show you what to do." Angelica pulled Lottie next to her, pushing Rose out of the way again. Rose felt upset, but Angelica didn't even notice.

7

Sophie tapped Rose on the shoulder. "You can stand next to me, if you like," she said. Rose smiled and stood next to Sophie. Just then, Miss Fontaine clapped her hands and the class began.

As the girls followed their teacher's graceful moves, Sophie gasped. Lottie was brilliant at dancing and Miss Fontaine noticed, too. She smiled as she saw how elegantly her new pupil danced. The girls in the class looked at each other in amazement. They could see that Lottie was just as good at ballet as Angelica. The problem was, Angelica could see it, too, and she was furious.

When the class was over, some of the girls crowded around Lottie. Everyone, that is, except Angelica, who stomped out, angrily. Lottie smiled politely and chatted for a while, then she went over to Sophie and Rose, who were standing together.

"I'm sorry you got pushed out of the way, Rose," said Lottie. Rose smiled at Lottie. "Don't worry," she replied. "Sophie has been really kind to me. Anyway, I'm fed up with Angelica bossing me around. It's time I found a new friend."

"I'll be your friend," said Sophie and Lottie, both at the same time. The three girls looked at each other and laughed.

The girls got on so well together that Rose invited them over to her house. They had lots of fun playing with her dressing-up box. Sophie pretended she was a pretty, pink fairy. Lottie was a princess and Rose was a prima ballerina. The friends spent the rest of the afternoon making up their own ballet stories, twirling and leaping across Rose's bedroom.

"This is fun," said Rose. "It's a shame Angelica isn't here to join in. Mind you, I think she's jealous of your dancing, Lottie, so maybe it's a good thing she isn't."

Lottie blushed. "Angelica just needs to realise that ballet class isn't about who's best. We should have fun and be friends. I'm sure she would be much happier if she relaxed a bit."

At the next ballet lesson, Lottie, Sophie and Rose stood together, chatting. Suddenly, Angelica came in. She looked annoyed that Rose had found new friends. She blamed Lottie for changing everything. "I'm the best ballerina in this class," she said to Lottie. "I'm not having that spoiled by you!"

"Yes, you are very good at ballet," replied Lottie, smiling. "I'm not here to spoil anything. I'm just here to dance and have fun with my friends."

Angelica looked surprised. She had expected Lottie to argue. With a toss of her dark curls, she stomped off towards the front of the class. However, she didn't see another girl, Jo, who was twirling around. Angelica bumped right into her and fell with a thump, onto the floor. "You're so clumsy, Jo," she shrieked. "You're like an elephant in a tutu!" All the other girls stopped and stared as poor Jo burst into tears.

Sophie stepped forward. "That was a very unkind thing to say," she said.
Angelica looked embarrassed. "Well, she should watch where she's going," she huffed.
"After all, I am the *best* ballerina."

"You may be very good at ballet," added Lottie. "But you aren't being very nice.
If you carry on this way, you won't have any friends."

Just then, Miss Fontaine clapped her hands and said that it was time to begin the class.

After the lesson, Angelica sat on her own, looking fed up. "Hey, cheer up!" said a voice. It was Lottie. Angelica looked up with tears in her eyes. "Everything was fine until you came along," she said. "Now I'm not the best anymore and you've taken my friend," she added, with a sniffle.

Lottie sat next to Angelica. "You don't need to keep telling everyone how good you are," she said. "Everyone knows you're a great dancer. There's no need for any of us to fall out. We can all be friends."

Angelica looked at Lottie and gave a small smile. "It's hard work being so bossy," she said. The other girls looked at each other and burst out laughing. They liked Angelica's sense of humor. Angelica felt happy. It was nice to have friends again. She promised that, from then on, they would all practice their dance steps happily and never, ever, fall out again.

New Slippers for Daisy

I t was time for Miss Sweet's ballet class. Daisy looked forward to it all week long. Her mum couldn't really afford the ballet lessons, so Daisy always made sure that she tried really hard whenever she danced. She wanted to make her mum proud.

As the class began, Daisy stretched up her arm and pointed her toes, as elegantly as she could. Then, suddenly, there was a ripping sound. Daisy looked down at her scuffed, old ballet slippers and cringed. One of them had torn and her toes were poking out from the hole. Some of the other girls giggled. "Never mind, Daisy," said Miss Sweet, kindly. "I'm sure your mother will buy you a nice new pair of ballet slippers."

Daisy didn't want to ask her mum for new ballet slippers. They were expensive and Mum didn't have any extra money. Daisy sat sadly at the edge of the class, watching the other girls dance. All the time, she thought about how she could get some new ballet slippers.

When it was time to get changed, Daisy opened the little purse in her kit bag. She had her lunch money, but a few coins would never be enough to buy the slippers. Sighing, she packed away and left, watched by the other girls who laughed and giggled together.

On the way home, Daisy walked past the dance shop. The window was full of beautiful ballet slippers, all in different colors. However, they were all far too expensive. "I wish I could afford to buy a pair," said Daisy, sadly, as tears trickled down her cheeks.

Suddenly, a kind voice said, "What's the matter, dear?" An old lady stood beside Daisy, holding out a tissue. Daisy blew her nose and then told the lady all about her torn ballet slippers. "I can't afford to buy new ones with my dinner money," she sniffled.

"Why don't you try *Wishes Emporium*," said the old lady, pointing down the road. "I'm sure you will find what you need there."

Daisy had never heard of Wishes Emporium before, but she thanked the little old lady and hurried off to find it.

Sure enough, further down the road was an old-fashioned shop, with a sign outside that said, *All your wishes come true at Wishes Emporium.*

Peering through the window, Daisy saw some dolls, old-fashioned toy cars and, in the middle, a lovely pair of ballet shoes. Her heart leapt. She quickly pushed the shop door, making the little shop bell jingle, noisily.

Inside the shop, an old man stood behind the counter. He smiled kindly at Daisy and said, "Have you come for these ballet shoes?"

"How did you know?" asked Daisy, staring at the white satin shoes, now resting on the counter. They weren't fancy, like the ones in the dance shop, but, as Daisy slipped them on her feet, it was almost as if they had been made for her. "How much are they?" she asked, nervously.

Daisy was amazed that the cost of the slippers was the exact amount that she had in her purse. She couldn't believe her luck.

When Daisy got home, she told her mum everything. "That's strange," said Mum. "I've never heard of that shop," she added, admiring the shoes. "I'm so glad you found nice new ballet slippers, though."

Daisy danced round and round, whirling and twirling like she had never done before. "Goodness me," said her mother, smiling. "You dance like a proper ballerina. I think those new shoes must be magic!"

The next week, in class, Daisy wore her new ballet shoes. As she danced, her feet felt as if they were floating across the floor. "Nice ballet shoes, Daisy," whispered one or two of the girls, smiling, as Daisy smiled shyly back.

Daisy danced so well, Miss Sweet was very impressed. "You're dancing beautifully, today, Daisy," she said, patting her arm as she walked past. "It must be those new slippers." Daisy had to agree. The slippers seemed almost magical and she felt lighter than air.

As time passed, Daisy's dancing got better and better, until she was Miss Sweet's star dancer. She always danced the lead whenever they put on a show, and with her special slippers, Daisy felt like a proper prima ballerina.

Daisy did go back and look for the Wishes Emporium, but, no matter how hard she tried, she never found it again. However, whenever she pirouetted across the dance studio, she said a silent, "thank you," for the shoes. With them, her dancing was magical!

Davina, Prima Ballerina

It was Lucy's first trip to the ballet with her dance school. Tonight, her heroine, the prima ballerina, Davina Dainty, was dancing the lead in Swan Lake. Lucy had been looking forward to it for weeks.

The performance would soon be starting and the theatre hummed with excitement. Lucy sat on the end of the front row with her friend, Chloe, next to their ballet teacher, Miss Tiptoe. "Do you think we'll meet Davina, afterwards?" she whispered.

Miss Tiptoe passed a bag of sweets along the row and whispered, "We'll make sure you get her autograph. Now, settle down and enjoy the show." Just then, the lights dimmed and everyone went quiet.

To Lucy's surprise, the curtain didn't move and the orchestra stayed silent. There was a long pause. Suddenly, a spotlight shone and a man in a suit walked onto the stage. Lucy and Chloe looked at one another. Something was wrong.

"Ladies and gentlemen," said the man. "I'm the manager and I have an announcement. I'm afraid Miss Davina Dainty is unable to perform tonight." A gasp of disappointment went through the crowd. "I know many of you have travelled here, especially to see Miss Dainty dance, but she's unwell. Her part will be danced by Suki Swann instead."

23

Lucy and Chloe felt very sad. They had waited so long for this evening. "Now I won't get Davina's autograph," said Lucy, fighting back her tears.

Miss Tiptoe leaned across and patted Lucy on the hand. "Never mind," she said, kindly. "Suki Swann is a brilliant dancer. We'll still enjoy the show."

Lucy, however, still felt upset. She'd been so excited about coming to see Davina and now the night was ruined. She sat, gloomily, as the orchestra began to play and the curtains drew back. Suki leaped, gracefully, into the centre of the stage. As she watched Suki dance, a tear ran down Lucy's cheek.

Miss Tiptoe leaned over to Lucy again, "She's very good, isn't she?" she whispered. Lucy nodded, but she wasn't really enjoying the performance. Secretly, she still wished it was Davina dancing.

The rest of the ballet passed by in a blur, as Lucy wondered if she'd ever get the chance to see her heroine on stage. When the curtain fell at the end of the performance, Chloe squeezed Lucy's arm. "Davina Dainty will always be my heroine, but Suki Swann is a fantastic dancer, too," she said. "Let's get her autograph."

Lucy just shook her head. She closed her autograph book. No autograph would be as good as Davina Dainty's.

Chloe and the other girls waited at the stage door, but Lucy hung back. Suddenly, Suki Swann appeared and the girls gathered round her, waving their autograph books.

When she'd signed all the books, Suki glanced up and saw Lucy leaning sadly against the wall. She was wondering why she looked so fed up, when Miss Tiptoe appeared.

As Miss Tiptoe and Suki spoke, Chloe hurried over to Lucy, waving her newly signed, autograph book. Together, they waited patiently for Miss Tiptoe. "I wonder what they are talking about?" said Chloe. "They've been chatting for ages."

Lucy wasn't bothered. Her big trip had been ruined and she just wanted to go home.

The next day, at ballet, all the girls could talk about was Swan Lake. Lucy didn't want to join in. She sat miserably on a bench waiting for the class to start. She wasn't even sure she felt like dancing.

The girls had been chatting for ages when Chloe said, "I wonder where Miss Tiptoe is?" Just then, she noticed a sign on the door that said, *Hi girls, I can't take the class today. I've arranged for some cover. Please warm up until they arrive. Miss Tiptoe.*

Chloe looked at Lucy. "I hope it's not bossy Miss Fogg again," she groaned. "She always shouts." Lucy just sighed. First she'd been let down by Davina and now Miss Tiptoe.

The girls were pointing their toes and stretching their arms up, when the doors swung open. Chloe, who had been expecting the dreaded Miss Fogg, gasped and nudged Lucy. The girls all stood open-mouthed, as a tall, graceful woman swept into the room. She was the most beautiful person Lucy had ever seen.

Lucy gasped. "It's Davina Dainty!" she cried, smiling for the first time since the ballet trip. She couldn't believe that her heroine was standing in front of her. The other girls bubbled with excitement, crowding around Davina, all of them speaking at once.

Just then, the doors to the class opened again and Miss Tiptoe walked in, grinning from ear to ear. "Settle down, girls," she laughed. "Give Davina some space."

Miss Tiptoe said, "I told Suki how upset you were when Davina couldn't dance. So, to make up for it, she asked Davina to come and take the class."

"Now, girls," said Davina, clapping her hands. "First position, please." The girls eagerly took their places and stood with their heels together. Davina walked round the class, giving the girls tips and praising them. When Lucy stretched her arms and Davina said, "Well done, that's lovely!" Lucy thought she would burst with happiness.

Lucy thought she'd never meet Davina, but here she was, signing her autograph book. Lucy's eyes sparkled, as she looked at the signature in the book. She'd met her heroine and even had a lesson with her. It was definitely the best day ever!

The Reluctant Ballerina

Georgie came rushing into the house, trailing mud everywhere. As usual, she was dressed in her football kit and it was very dirty. Georgie's mum was not happy to see mucky footprints all over her clean kitchen floor.

"Right, that's it, Georgie West. No more football!" she said. "I've signed you up for some ballet classes with Miss Honey. It's time you did something ladylike for once."

Georgie groaned. She hated doing girly things. She'd much rather be outside, riding her bike, or kicking a football around. However, no matter how much Georgie pleaded, her mum insisted she give ballet a try.

Georgie's mum took her to buy a ballet outfit. "Yuck!" cried Georgie, as she tried on a pink leotard. "I'm not wearing this. I look really stupid and I *hate* pink!"

Eventually, after much fussing, Georgie's mum persuaded her to choose a white ballet kit. "At least it's not pink," said Georgie, gloomily. Then, as they left the shop, Georgie had an idea. She would take the ballet kit to class, but it didn't mean she had to wear it.

Ballet Bags

forms

On the afternoon of the class, Mum dropped Georgie off at Miss Honey's dance school. Inside, Georgie looked at the other girls. They all looked neatly dressed and were busy chatting about clothes and boy bands. Georgie just wanted to be playing football. She didn't belong here. It was far too girly.

Then, Georgie slipped off her jeans and top. Underneath, she was wearing her football kit! There was no way she was going to put on a stupid leotard. Some of the other girls pointed and giggled, but Georgie didn't care. She was sure Miss Honey would see she wasn't interested in ballet, then she wouldn't have to come anymore.

Miss Honey came to see what all the fuss was about. Georgie explained that she didn't want to be at ballet class, she just wanted to play football. Miss Honey smiled, kindly. "Why don't you put your ballet slippers on and have a go," she said. "Who knows, you might like it!"

Reluctantly, Georgie put the ballet slippers on and stood at the back of the class. Music started to play and the girls followed Miss Honey's movements. Georgie was amazed at how graceful they looked.

"Hi, there," whispered a girl standing next to Georgie. She had lovely, brown curly hair. "I'm Jo. I love football, too. I play for the Town Tornadoes and come to ballet to strengthen my legs. It's really improved my game."

Georgie was really impressed. It was her dream to play for the Town Tornadoes. Could ballet really make her play football better, she wondered? If it was good enough for Jo, it was good enough for her.

Georgie concentrated hard for the rest of the class. She tried to copy Jo's graceful movements and listened carefully to Miss Honey's instructions. When Mum came to pick her up, Georgie told her all about Jo and how dancing had helped her football game. Her mum smiled. Trust Georgie to find someone who was football mad!

From then on, Georgie and Jo were best friends. They practised their ballet steps and played football together. In no time, Georgie was very good at ballet. Now all of her movements were graceful and she loved leaping high into the air, stretching her legs and pointing her toes. Georgie noticed her legs were getting stronger and she was able to run and kick better than ever at football.

One day, Georgie and Jo were messing about. "Look, I'm a football ballerina!" joked Georgie. "Actually, I think you're ready for the team try-outs," replied Jo. Georgie's heart leapt. "Do you really think I'm good enough to play for the *Town Tornadoes?*" Jo smiled and nodded. "Try-outs are on Saturday morning. Don't be late!"

On Saturday, Georgie arrived at the football ground. She felt really nervous. Suddenly, she saw Miss Honey and the other girls from her class on the sidelines. She smiled when Miss Honey waved and called, "We've come to cheer you on. Good luck!"

It was a fast game, but Georgie ran like the wind. She was determined to make the team. "She looks so elegant," said Miss Honey. "Look, she's scored a goal!" Everyone clapped and cheered.

After the game, the coach told Georgie that she'd made the team. She couldn't believe it. Georgie hugged Jo and said, "It's all thanks to ballet making my legs strong." "I guess you'll be giving up ballet, now?" said Miss Honey, sadly. Georgie just shook her head. "I'll be back, Miss Honey," she promised. Georgie loved football, but she'd grown to love the graceful movements of ballet, too.

Miss Honey smiled. She had a feeling that her reluctant ballerina would be dancing for a long time to come.

Ballet School in Trouble

Miss Ribbon's School of Ballet had seen better days. It was in a run-down part of town and badly in need of repair. However, Evie and all her ballet class friends loved going there. Their teacher, Miss Ribbon, was very kind and they all enjoyed dancing.

One afternoon, Evie was warming up, when Miss Ribbon came in looking pale and worried. She clapped her hands and asked the class to listen carefully. "Girls, I have bad news," she said. "As you know, this building is very old. Now, the roof is leaking and I don't have enough money to fix it. I'm really sorry, but the school will have to close."

The girls were shocked. Some of them burst into tears. Evie walked over to Miss Ribbon and held her hand. There were tears in her teacher's eyes. "Miss Ribbon, there must be something we can do," said Evie, gently. Miss Ribbon dabbed her eyes. "I'm afraid not," she sniffled. Evie looked at her friend, Sarah. "We have to do something," she whispered.

Evie thought for a moment. "I know," she said, suddenly. "Why don't we hold a charity sale here, this Saturday? I'll do some leaflets and we can collect things to sell.

Miss Ribbon and the girls thought this was a brilliant idea. They all gathered round to chat about what stalls they could run.

The next day, Evie and Sarah posted leaflets through letterboxes and collected things to sell. At the end of the road, they came to Mrs Crabbe's house. Sarah looked a bit scared. "Let's not go to Mrs Crabbe's," she said. "She's so grumpy."

"I'm not scared of her," said Evie and she marched right up to the front door and knocked on it several times.

A tall woman with grey hair flung the door open, "What do you want?" she said, sharply." Evie tried to explain, but the woman said, "No, thank you!" then slammed the door shut. "How rude!" said Evie, crossly. She grabbed a leaflet from the pile she was holding and scribbled a note on the back. Then, she stuffed it through Mrs Crabbe's letterbox.

The next morning, at the ballet school, the girls set their stalls out early. Sarah's mum had made loads of cakes and Evie sold some raffle tickets. Soon, people started to come into the studio and buy things. In no time at all it got quite busy. Evie rattled her raffle ticket tin. "My tin's filling up. I do hope we make enough to fix the roof," she said.

When the sale was over Miss Ribbon shut the doors and flopped into a chair. "Phew," she said. "What a day! Let's clear up and count the money."

The girls tidied away the tables and swept up tickets and cake wrappers. Then, Evie, Sarah and Miss Ribbon sat at a table, sorting coins into piles. Miss Ribbon counted all the money and then she gave a long sigh. "I'm sorry, girls," she said, sadly. "You've all worked so hard, but we haven't raised enough to fix the roof."

Evie was heart-broken. "We have done all this for nothing," she said.

Suddenly, the door swung open and a tall, grey-haired woman swept in. It was Mrs Crabbe! "Can I help you?" said Miss Ribbon, dabbing her eyes.
"No, but I think I can help you," replied Mrs Crabbe. She handed Miss Ribbon an old photograph of a woman with a little girl in a ballet outfit.

Miss Ribbon gasped. "That woman is my mother," she said. "Who is the little girl, beside her?"
"That's me," replied Mrs Crabbe, smiling. "Your mother was my teacher. I have very happy memories of dancing at this school. That's why I want to save it. I'll pay for your roof."

Evie and Sarah looked at Mrs Crabbe. She must have read Evie's note. Now she was going to save the school. Maybe Mrs Crabbe wasn't so grumpy and scary after all.

43

Mrs Crabbe and Miss Ribbon organized all the repairs for the ballet school. Soon, the hole in the roof had gone and the walls had been painted. Everything gleamed and the ballet studio looked like new.

On the day of the grand re-opening, Miss Ribbon and the girls put on a show in honor of Mrs Crabbe. "Thank you very much for saving our school," said Miss Ribbon. "Thank Evie and Sarah," replied Mrs Crabbe. "Evie's note was so enthusiastic. It made me remember how important ballet was to me."

"I'm so glad I wrote that note," said Evie. "It saved our school and we cheered up Mrs Crabbe, too!" Mrs Crabbe had to agree. She looked as happy now as she had as a little girl in the old photo, which now had pride of place on the studio wall.

After that, Evie and her classmates never had to worry about a leaking roof again. With Mrs Crabbe to help them, Miss Ribbon's school would never, ever be a ballet school in trouble.

45

Old School, New School

Grace stood outside a tall, elegant building. She felt very nervous. Grace still couldn't believe that she was starting lessons here, at the best ballet school in town. Thanks to her mum's new job, they finally could afford the classes. Her friends at her old ballet school had been very envious when they found out. Everyone wanted to dance at The Central School of Ballet.

However, Grace missed her old ballet school and all her friends. She thought about her ballet teacher, Miss Golightly, and how much fun her lessons had been. Would it be the same here? Grace took a deep breath. She would soon find out. Opening the door, she stepped inside.

It was very quiet in the studio. No one said hello to Grace as she came in. Girls just changed, silently, folding their clothes in neat, little piles. One or two whispered, quietly, to each other. It was very different to Grace's old class, where everyone bustled about, laughing and joking, as they got ready.

Grace quietly slipped on her leotard and tights. She was putting on her ballet shoes when she realized that a couple of the girls were whispering and sniggering at her. Compared to their smart outfits, Grace's leotard looked old and bobbly and her shoes were scuffed and frayed. "You better change those for the next class," hissed one girl. "Miss Sharp won't let you dance in scruffy gear."

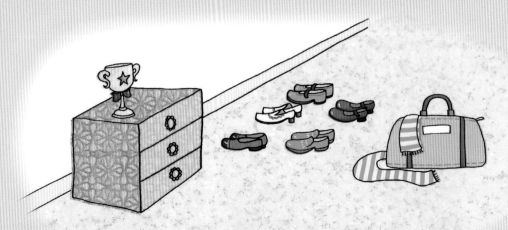

47

Before Grace could answer, the door swung open and Miss Sharp appeared. She was a tall, serious-looking woman with grey hair, pinned up in a bun. The girls hurried to their positions at the barre, followed by Grace.

"New girl, come here!" barked Miss Sharpe. Grace shuffled forward. Miss Sharp looked her up and down, with her eyes narrowed and her lips pursed. "How dare you turn up to my class in such shabby kit," she sniffed. "Be sure to replace it for next week."

Grace blinked back tears as she took her place at the barre. Suddenly, she longed to be back in Miss Golightly's class, where it didn't matter what you wore, as long as you had fun.

As the class went on, Grace couldn't believe how strict it was. The atmosphere was tense, as everyone tried to follow Miss Sharp's orders. Every so often, she would stop the lesson to single someone out, telling them their footwork was sloppy or their arms weren't straight. Each time, she made the class go back to the beginning. Everyone groaned, inwardly, as they began again for what seemed like the twentieth time.

Grace was terrified that Miss Sharp would pick on her again, so she tried her best to copy the moves. However, sure enough, Miss Sharp singled her out. "New girl. Your posture is terrible. You'll need to work harder if you want to dance at my school!" she snapped.

49

As Grace got changed, her lip wobbled. She wasn't used to such a strict teacher. On top of this, no one in the class had spoken to her. She wasn't sure she wanted to come back to ballet again. Sadly, she left the building alone and walked home.

When Grace got home, she flopped down on the sofa, next to her mum. Everything ached and Grace had never felt so tired. "Did you enjoy your new ballet school?" asked her mum.

Sighing heavily, Grace told her all about Miss Sharp telling her off and how bossy and nasty she was. "I don't think I want to dance anymore," Grace said, miserably.

"The thing is, I've paid for the term," said her mum, frowning. "Besides, you love ballet. You can't let someone like Miss Sharp stop you."

50

For the rest of the week, no matter how hard Grace's mum tried to persuade her, Grace didn't want to give ballet another chance. The thought of going back to Miss Sharp's class filled her with dread. She would rather give up her beloved ballet altogether than go back to that horrible school.

On ballet day, Grace's mum was waiting in the car with her kit. Grace opened the door and cried, "Please don't make me go back!"
Grace's mum looked serious and said, "Sorry, Grace, but I've paid until the end of term. Can you stick it out? For me?"

Grace knew Miss Sharp would be nagging her and picking holes in her dancing, but she couldn't let her mum pay for classes she didn't go to, so she reluctantly got in the car.

Grace was so busy dreading the hour ahead that she didn't notice when the car stopped. She got out and was surprised when her best friend, Suzy, appeared. "Hiya, Grace, I'm so glad you're back!" she called. Grace snapped out of her bad mood and looked around her. This wasn't Miss Sharp's School. It was Miss Golightly's!

Grace hugged Suzy and she rushed through the double doors, into the noise and bustle of the studio. Inside, girls were chattering, noisily, as they rummaged in bags and put on their leotards. Suzy was singing as she got changed. Grace laughed as she looked around. It was so much nicer than the stressful silence at Miss Sharp's school.

When Miss Golightly appeared, Grace threw her arms round her. Mrs Golightly laughed and said, "Welcome back, Grace. I'm so pleased your mum got her money back from Miss Sharp. After all, ballet should be fun, not frightening."

For the rest of the class, Grace danced, happily, next to Suzy. As she pointed her toes and held up her arms, Miss Golightly patted her arm and said, "Lovely dear. You're doing brilliantly!"

Who needed a posh ballet school when you could come to Mrs Golightly's class? She made ballet so enjoyable and everyone loved her. Grace knew she was back where she belonged and that her old school was the best, ever.

53

The Magic Music Box

It was past midnight, but Holly couldn't sleep. She tossed and turned, pulling the duvet around her, but it was no use. All she could think about was her ballet exam. It was only a week away and Holly still hadn't learned all the steps. She thought of her last ballet class. What a disaster that had been. She felt such a fool for falling over during her pirouette.

Holly got out of bed and walked over to the window. The night sky glowed with stars. It looked magical. A soft beam of moonlight shone on the lovely, elegant ballerina on Holly's jewelry box. "Oh, how I wish I could look as beautiful as her," she sighed.

Suddenly, outside, a shooting star streaked across the sky. Holly quickly made a wish. "Please let me pass my exam," she whispered. Suddenly, the music box began to play its soft, tinkling tune and the ballerina turned slowly around. "Wow!" said Holly. "How did that happen? It really must be magic!"

Holly snuggled down into her duvet and fell into a wonderful sleep. In her dreams, the beautiful ballerina stepped off her music box and showed Holly how to dance like a graceful, prima ballerina.

Later that day, after school, Holly was changing for ballet. She told her friend, Amber, all about the strange dream she'd had. "Imagine if your music box could come to life, it would be so cool!" smiled Amber.

When the class started, Holly's teacher, Miss Ayres, took them through the steps for their ballet exam. Holly's legs shook at the mere mention of the exam. She tried to copy her teacher's moves, but she seemed to get it all wrong. "If I'm this nervous in class," she thought, "how on earth will I get through the exam?"

Just then, Holly thought of the little ballerina on the music box. To her surprise, as the class wore on, she found it easier to remember the steps. Suddenly, she felt better. However, when she thought of the exam, it all went horribly wrong. Yet again, Holly tripped over when it came to the pirouette. She landed with a bump, blushing furiously, as her classmates giggled. She'd never learn how to do it before the exam.

After class, Holly practiced her steps. Just like before, she did everything perfectly until she thought of the exam. Then, she lost her balance and fell. *I'm going to need all the help I can get*, thought Holly, looking at her music box.

That night, Holly dreamed she was dancing with the ballerina. Together, they whirled and twirled around the room. Holly felt lighter than air, as she effortlessly spun into a perfect, whirling pirouette.

Suddenly, Holly woke up. She gazed at the motionless figure on top of her music box. Had she really been dancing with her? It seemed so real, but Holly knew it was only a dream.

Over the next few days, Holly practised, as hard as she could. However, whenever she thought of the exam, her tummy knotted up and her legs shook.

The night before her exam, Holly drifted into a nervous sleep. Just like before, the ballerina stepped down from the music box. This time, however, she took Holly on a magical dance around the moon and the stars. They whirled and twirled through the enchanted night sky and Holly felt as light as air.

"Holly, you know the ballet steps," said the ballerina. "So, reach for the stars!" Then, she plucked a star from the sky and pressed it into Holly's hand. "This is for luck," she whispered.

Drrring, drrring! The alarm clock rang. Holly jolted awake. She had been dreaming again and it seemed so real. Then, Holly noticed she was gripping something in her hand. Looking down, she saw a star-shaped hairslide, glittering in the morning sunlight. Holly was amazed. However, she couldn't think about that now. She had a ballet exam to do.

At the exam, Holly was almost ready. She couldn't help but feel nervous as she tried to stuff her clothes into her practise bag. Fumbling, she dropped the bag on the floor and her belongings scattered everywhere. Holly scrabbled about, trying to find them all.

"Here, you dropped this," said Amber. Holly was startled, as she took the glittering hairclip from her friend. As Miss Ayres clapped her hands, Holly quickly clipped the slide in her hair. She closed her eyes and remembered the ballerina's words, "You must believe in yourself…"

Stepping onto the dance floor, Holly pretended she was back in her bedroom, dancing at night with the ballerina.

To Holly's surprise, she danced effortlessly. Even her pirouette was perfect! Her classmates gasped as they watched her twirl and spin. They could hardly believe how much Holly had changed. She was no longer clumsy and nervous. Now, she danced like a prima ballerina.

Miss Ayres presented her with a certificate and medal. "Well done, Holly, you've passed with top marks!" she said. Holly felt very proud. She would never have believed a week ago that she could pass, let alone do so well.

Clutching her medal, Holly touched the hair slide. Was it a dream, or had she really danced with the ballerina each night? Holly wasn't sure, but she was glad that wishing on a star had made her dreams come true.

Anna's Audition

It was the day of Anna's audition for the Lightfoot School of Dance. She was about to leave for the bus, when her dad ran downstairs and grabbed his car keys from the shelf. "Come on, Anna," he said. "Let's get going, or you'll be late."

"Don't worry, Dad," said Anna. "I'll get the bus. It stops right outside the school." However, her dad insisted, "Nonsense. It's no trouble," he said. "Anyway, what if the bus doesn't come? I know how much this day means to you."

The car edged slowly through the traffic. Anna swallowed nervously. Her tummy was fluttering with nerves. She closed her eyes and went through her steps one more time. She knew in her heart that she would dance well, as long as her anxiety didn't get the better of her.

A sudden beeping interrupted her thoughts. Anna's eye snapped open. Her dad pulled over to the side of the road and flipped the bonnet open. "What's wrong?" cried Anna. "I'm sorry, Anna," replied Dad. "The car's broken down. You'll have to get the bus," he sighed, handing Anna some change. "Good luck!"

Now Anna was feeling really nervous. She had to make the audition. At the bus stop, she frowned when she saw the crowd of people waiting. By the grumpy looks on their faces, they'd been there some time.

"I've been standing here for half an hour," grumbled an old lady. She took out a pair of reading glasses and peered at the timetable. "Must be those road works," she complained.

Anna couldn't believe her bad luck. First, the car had broken down and now the bus was late. She knew that Miss Lightfoot didn't allow latecomers to audition. It seemed that all her dreams were slipping away.

Anna looked down the road, anxiously, for any sign of the bus. Then, she noticed a young woman crossing the road with a pram.

Anna watched as the woman struggled to lift the pram up the kerb. "Here, let me help you," she said, smiling kindly at the woman, who looked exhausted.
"Oh, thank you," replied the woman, smiling. "Just those steps to go now," she added, nodding her head towards some concrete steps, outside a block of flats.

Anna looked up the road again. There was still no sign of the bus. "I'll give you a hand," she offered.

The woman smiled, gratefully, as Anna helped her to lift the buggy up the steps. Anna was just passing her the last two shopping bags when, to her horror, she heard the hiss of a door closing and turned to see her bus pulling away from the kerb. "No!" she wailed, hurrying down the steps and waving frantically at the driver. It was no use, though. The bus had gone.

Sadly, Anna flopped down on the kerb. Her dreams were in tatters. Now she would never get the chance to audition for Miss Lightfoot. A tear slid down her cheek, followed by another, then another. "It's so unfair," she muttered, crying.

"What is?" said a voice. Anna turned to see the young woman she'd helped standing beside her with a concerned look on her face. She smiled and handed Anna a tissue. Before Anna could help herself, the whole story of her disastrous morning came tumbling out.

The woman listened while Anna spoke. "Now I'll never dance at the Lightfoot School of Dance!" she sobbed. "Well, I think you deserve another chance," said the young woman, firmly. "You only missed your bus because you were helping me. I'll see what I can do," she said.

Anna didn't see how the young woman could help her now. She'd blown her only chance. As Anna made her way home, she felt very unhappy.

Later that morning, the phone rang. "It's Miss Lightfoot," said her dad. Anna trembled. She hoped she wasn't going to get shouted at for missing the audition.

"Anna Wallace?" enquired Miss Lightfoot. "I want you to come and audition. Try not to miss your bus," she added, firmly. Anna shrieked and leaped around the room. She couldn't believe she was getting another chance!

That afternoon, Anna's tummy fluttered as she stood before the great Miss Lightfoot. She was tall and elegant, with half-moon glasses perched on the end of her nose. Anna felt quite intimidated. Shutting her eyes, she composed herself. She couldn't afford to wreck her chances this time. As the music started, Anna's nerves melted away and she danced elegantly and gracefully.

Miss Lightfoot watched her, intently, but halfway through, she held up her hand and said, "That's enough, Anna. I'm glad I gave you a second chance. You dance beautifully. You've won a place."

Anna beamed with pride. "Thank you!" she cried. "Why did you give me a second chance?" she asked, puzzled.
"The woman you helped, phoned me," said Miss Lightfoot, smiling. "When she told me how kind you were, I felt you deserved it. After all, one good turn deserves another."

As Anna made her way home, she thought it was funny how things had turned out. Who would have thought that her worst day would turn out to be her best as well?

Rosie's Wish

Rosie pulled on her purple leotard and sat on the dance floor, next to her best friend, Molly. They were waiting for their teacher, Miss Plum, to make an announcement. "What do you think it's about?" hissed Rosie in Molly's ear.

However, before Molly could answer, Miss Plum clapped her hands and said, "Settle down girls. As you know, the Russian Ballet is in town next week for a one-off show. I've managed to get tickets for their performance and will be raffling a pair at next week's ballet class."

Miss Plum paused and smiled, as a ripple of excitement went through the class. Rosie squeezed her eyes shut and made a silent wish, "Please, let it be me who wins the raffle."

Clearing her throat, Miss Plum grinned and added, "Make sure you bring your purses next week. All proceeds from the raffle will go towards the ballet school." With that, she clapped her hands again and everyone took their positions to begin their warm up.

For the rest of the class, all Rosie could think about were the tickets. She wanted to buy as many as she could, but she knew her mum and dad didn't have much money. Then, suddenly, Rosie had a brilliant idea.

That evening, when she got home, Rosie rushed up to her pretty, pink bedroom and pulled out a notebook. She scribbled, hurriedly, then quickly tore the page out of her book and dashed downstairs to find her mum. She showed her the list she had written and said, "Mum, if I do these chores for you, will you pay me?"

Her mum peered at the list and smiled. "Well, your prices seem reasonable and I could always do with a hand." Mum handed Rosie the yellow washing up gloves and said, "Why don't you start by washing the car?"

For the rest of the week, Rosie did as many chores as she could for her mum, dad and the neighbors. She watched in satisfaction as the pile of money grew larger every day.

72

On raffle night, Rosie carefully tipped out her money jar and counted the coins. She worked out that she had earned enough money to buy twenty raffle tickets. Surely that would be enough?

Carefully, Rosie tipped the money back into the jar and slipped it in to her practice bag. Crossing her fingers for luck, she wished again, "Please let me pick the winning ticket," she said, to no one in particular.

At the dance studio, Rosie arrived to find a queue of girls already crowded around Miss Plum in a ticket-buying frenzy.

73

When it was her turn, Rosie tipped the contents of her money jar into Miss Plum's cash box. "My goodness, Rosie," she laughed. "You are keen." She handed Rosie twenty yellow tickets and whispered, "Good luck!"

After a while, Miss Plum produce a battered old, red felt hat with a flourish. "Time to pick the winner!" she cried, as a cheer went round the room. Rosie closed her eyes and wished as hard as she could. "Please, let it be me!" she whispered, crossing her fingers again for luck.

Miss Plum moved her hand around, inside the hat. It seemed that everyone in the room was holding their breath. "The winner is..." she called, pulling out a raffle ticket, "... blue 185." Tears stung Rosie's eyes. None of her yellow tickets had won.

All Rosie's hard work had been in vain. She was so upset that, at first, she didn't notice Molly waving a blue ticket.

"It's me! It's me! I can't believe it!" cried Molly, running forward. She turned to smile at Rosie, but seeing her downcast face, Molly's grin faded. As Miss Plum handed her the gold envelope, she whispered something to her. Miss Plum nodded, then called Rosie over.

Molly smiled and said to her, "Rosie, I want you to have the other ticket. Miss Plum already has her ticket, so she can take us."

Rosie's eyes widened. She hugged Molly gratefully and cried, "Thank you!"

For the rest of the week, all Rosie could think about was her night at the ballet.
Molly had invited her over for dinner and when the night of the show finally arrived,
she hurried over to Molly's house. Together, the friends chattered away as they picked at
their food. It was the first time they'd seen a ballet at the theatre and they were both far
too excited to eat.

At 6 o'clock, Miss Plum arrived in her little, red car to pick them up. Rosie's tummy
was gurgling with excitement as the car pulled into a parking space opposite the theater.

They settled into the deep, velvet seats, enjoying the atmosphere of the theater.
All around them, people were talking in hushed voices as the orchestra tuned up.

As the lights dimmed and the orchestra began to play, Rosie squeezed her friend's arm. She was bubbling with excitement. The dancers leaped onto the stage, moving like graceful butterflies. Rosie thought they were the most wonderful ballerinas she'd ever seen.

The friends were so wrapped up in the dancing that it was a surprise when the lights went up and the interval was announced. "I'm having the best time," Rosie whispered to Molly, her eyes sparkling. "I've never seen anything so amazing. They dance like beautiful birds."

Rosie smiled. She may not have won the raffle, but thanks to Molly, her wonderful, kind best friend, her wish had still come true. Settling down to watch the rest of the show, Rosie felt like the luckiest girl in the world.

Lily the Ballet Star

It was Lily's last day at Miss Shine's Dance School. She stood, quietly, watching as her friends flitted across the familiar studio, like delicate butterflies. Lily had been coming here for a long time. However, she had reached the highest grade and it was time to go to a more advanced school. Lily would miss everyone, especially Miss Shine. She was a lovely teacher and it was thanks to her patience and encouragement that Lily had done so well.

Lily's best friend, Alice, bounded over and threw her arms around her. "I can't believe you won't be here next week!" she cried, hugging her tightly. "I'll miss you *so much!*"

Lily did her best to smile at Alice but, inside, she felt very sad indeed.

Lily was going to the famous Prima Ballet School and she was really nervous. What if she wasn't good enough or no one would be her friend?

Suddenly, Miss Shine clapped her hands together and said. "As you know, it's Lily's last day." She held out a pretty, pink box with a silver ribbon tied around it. "This is for you, Lily, with our love," she said, pressing the box into Lily's hand. "If you ever feel alone, touch it and remember to believe in yourself."

Lily opened the box and her eyes welled with tears. Inside, nestled on a pink velvet pad, was a silver ballet slipper on a delicate chain. As Lily whispered, "Thank you," a little sob escaped from her lips.

The days flew by and soon Lily found herself outside the big, red brick building of the Prima Ballet School. Touching her necklace for luck, she went inside.

Lily was swept along a corridor in a crowd of chattering girls who were hurrying to their next class. Stopping for a moment outside the studio door, Lily took a deep breath, then went inside. Girls were already dancing and Lily gasped, as she watched them gliding across the floor like beautiful swans. "That's amazing," she said.

"I'm not sure I'll ever be that good," said a voice. Lily turned round to see a friendly-looking girl, with red hair and freckles, smiling at her. "Hello, I'm Jenny. Are you new, too?" she asked. Lily was pleased that she wasn't the only new girl. Together, she and Jenny found a place at the back and warmed up.

Lily puffed her way through the class. It was a lot tougher than Miss Shine's ballet lessons and her legs ached as she bent her knees and pointed her toes, for what seemed like the hundredth time.

Jenny was finding the steps difficult, too. "Ouch!" she said, as she leaned on the barre and felt a sharp twinge in her leg. "Oh, dear," moaned Jenny. "I just can't seem to get it right. I never had any problem at my old ballet school."

Lily and Jenny watched the other girls in the class as they glided around, leaping and twirling. *They make it look so easy,* thought Lily. *I will have to work really hard to be as good as they are.* Lily held the little silver necklace that Miss Shine had given to her. *I've just got to believe in myself,* she thought.

Over the next few weeks, Lily worked really hard at her ballet. One day, she was chatting to Jenny, when a girl from their class came up to them. "Hi, my name's Jane," she said. "I just wanted to say that I think you are both doing really well."

Jane invited Lily and Jenny to go for a milkshake. She told them that soon the show list would be going up for the end of term performance. "Keep any eye out for it," she said. "You might get parts."

Just as Jane had said, at the next class, the show list was put up. Lily was delighted to see that Jenny was dancing in the show and, even more amazingly, Lily had a solo part!

Over the next few weeks, Lily was so nervous that even Jenny couldn't keep her calm. She spent every spare moment practicing her steps.

On the night of the show, Lily felt incredibly nervous. "I don't think I can do this," she said to Jenny, in the changing rooms. "I'm just not ready!"
"Come on," said Jenny, giving Lily a squeeze. "You'll be okay. Think how far we've come," she added.

Lily went onto the stage and peered through the gap in the curtains. Her stomach quivered with nerves. Touching her necklace, Lily remembered Miss Shine's words. She had to believe in herself. So, taking a deep breath, Lily took her place in the wings, as the orchestra began to play. She gulped as the curtain went up. It was show time!

Lily listened carefully for her cue. Holding her arms out, she leaped onto stage, twirling her way through her steps perfectly. Her nerves had melted away, and as she danced, Lily felt really proud. She thought back to her first day at the Prima Ballet School. It seemed a long time ago now.

Spinning into a final pirouette, Lily brought her hands together above her head and held her pose. As she listened to the the audience clapping and cheering, Lily thought she would burst with happiness. Blinking in the bright lights, she noticed someone was waving. It was Miss Shine and Alice! Lily realised that all her friends from her old school had come to see her dance. She blushed as Alice threw roses onto the stage.

Backstage, Jenny and Lily hugged one another. "We did it!" cried Lily.
Just then, Alice and Miss Shine appeared. Alice was beaming. "You danced
like a proper ballerina," she said. Miss Shine smiled at Lily. "I'm sure that, one day,
you'll be a prima ballerina, Lily," she added, proudly.

Lily looked at Miss Shine and touched the necklace. "I've worn my necklace every
day," she said. "It has helped me, so much. Whenever I felt scared, I remembered your
advice. It is important to work hard, but above all, it is important to believe in yourself.
I did and now I really do feel like Lily the ballet star!"

Stage Fright

Fleur carefully pulled her long hair back off her face and wound it into a neat bun. Clipping it tightly in place, she checked her costume in the dressing room mirror. It was the dress rehearsal for their performance of Copelia and Fleur was feeling very nervous.

Fleur fluffed up the delicate net on her pink tutu, took a deep breath, then opened the door and headed for the wings. She took her place at the side of the stage and waited for the music to start. Her legs were so wobbly that she wasn't sure she could dance.

86

"I can't do this," Fleur whispered to herself, as her tummy jumped with nerves. Suddenly, a voice said, "Of course you can!" Startled, Fleur turned to find herself face to face with a girl about the same age as her. She was pale, with silvery hair and a long, white ballet outfit that looked a bit old fashioned. "You made me jump," said Fleur. "Where did you come from?"

The girl smiled and said, softly, "I'm Sarah. I'm always around when people need me. Don't be scared. I'll stay and watch you dance. You'll be fine."

Just then, Fleur heard her cue. Amazingly, her nerves had vanished. She danced, nimbly, onto the stage, with her head held high and her arms stretched out. All the time, Sarah watched from the wings.

Fleur felt strangely comforted by Sarah's presence and she danced beautifully, feeling confident and relaxed. It felt as though she'd only been on stage for moments when her dance was over. Padding back to the wings, Fleur looked for Sarah to thank her. *That's odd*, she thought, feeling puzzled. *How did she disappear so quickly?*

Shrugging her shoulders, Fleur hurried back to the dressing room. Perhaps she'd find Sarah there. She opened the door and scanned the bustling room. Everywhere she looked, girls were chattering happily as they changed, but there was no sign of Sarah.

Fleur sat down and untied the pink satin ribbons on her ballet shoes, thinking about how kind Sarah had been to her. But who was she?

Just then, Miss Satin, swept into the room. "Well done!" she cried. "You were all wonderful. You danced like angels!" She waved a hand at Fleur and smiled broadly. "You, my dear, were fabulous!" she said, giving Fleur's arm a squeeze. "If you carry on dancing like that, you'll be off to the Royal Ballet School before long. Now, home to bed, everyone. I want you all to have an early night ready for the big show," she said, ushering the girls out like an anxious mother hen.

The next evening, Fleur felt nervous again as she cycled to the theater. Her tummy rumbled and she felt sick every time she thought about dancing in front of so many people. She hoped Sarah would be waiting in the wings again, as the mysterious girl had really calmed her nerves while she danced.

Inside, Fleur found Miss Satin fussing around her classmates, adjusting their buns and helping some of the younger girls put their tutus on. "Ahhh, our star performer!" she boomed, taking Fleur to a free spot in the corner of the dressing room. "Come along now. It won't be long till curtain up," she added, handing Fleur her costume.

It seemed like only moments until Fleur was backstage, listening to the orchestra as they began to play the opening bars of the music. Her cue was moments away. She squeezed her eyes shut and willed her legs to stop shaking. "If only Sarah was here," she muttered.

"Just as well I am," said a voice. Fleur whirled round and she saw Sarah sitting behind her. "I'm so glad to see you!" gabbled Fleur, her nerves melting away as she saw Sarah's reassuring smile. "Will you stay and watch again?"
Sarah nodded. "I'm always here when performers need me," she grinned as Fleur heard her cue.

Fleur felt calm as she held her head high and leapt onto the stage. She twirled and whirled through her dance, moving elegantly and gracefully across the stage. She felt as light as air, as she leaped up high. Meanwhile, in the wings, Sarah watched her every move.

All too soon, the dance was over. Fleur gave a low curtsey, then made her way off stage. She thought she would burst with pride as she listened to the audience cheering madly and shouting, "Bravo!"

Fleur slipped into the wings and was pleased to see that this time, Sarah had waited for her. "You were brilliant. I wish it had been me out there, dancing," said Sarah, sadly.

Fleur sat down next to Sarah. She was just about to thank her, when Miss Satin appeared. "That was superb," she said.

Fleur blushed. "I couldn't have done it without Sarah," she said, turning to her new friend. However, to Fleur's surprise, Sarah had disappeared.
"So, you've met our resident ghost," said Miss Satin, smiling. "She always appears when a dancer has stage fright. I hope she didn't scare you?"

Fleur smiled at Miss Satin. "No, it's comforting to know she's here. If I ever have stage fright again, I'll know exactly who to call on."

Ruby Saves the Show

It was the Saturday before the big ballet show. Ella, the lead dancer, was pirouetting across her living room, as her best friend, Ruby, watched her closely. "That's it, Ella, but you need to hold your arms a little higher," Ruby said.

Ella smiled gratefully at her friend. Ruby was so shy in class and always hid away at the back, but she listened really carefully to their teacher, Miss Petticoat, and picked up new steps really quickly. Ella was surprised that Ruby wasn't in the show. It seemed a shame that she stayed in the shadows. "You know me," said Ruby. "I'm just too shy."

The girls spent the rest of the day practicing together. Ella was feeling really nervous about her solo, but as usual, Ruby knew just the right thing to say. "You'll be fine," she said. "You know all the steps now and I think you'll do brilliantly."

Ruby really believed that Ella would do well. However, she was a bit concerned that Ella kept sneezing. By the end of the afternoon, Ella didn't look well at all. "You're very pale," said Ruby, as Ella rubbed her eyes, sleepily.

Suddenly, Ella gave a huge sneeze. "I'm just tired," she said, blowing her nose. "Don't worry. I'll see you at ballet tomorrow," she added, as she showed Ruby to the front door.

The next day, Ruby arrived early at their ballet class. She was surprised to find that Ella wasn't there. *That's odd,* she thought. *I'm sure we said we'd meet early to practice.*

Ruby found a spot at the side of the room and began her warm-up stretches. She hadn't done much at all when Miss Petticoat rushed into the room. To her surprise, her teacher, who was usually so calm and composed, looked panicked and stressed. She cleared her throat nervously, then called the girls into a circle. "I'm afraid I have some rather disappointing news," she said. "I've just heard from Ella's mum that she is ill. She's sent me a note."

While Miss Petticoat rummaged in her bag for her reading glasses, a murmur went round the room. Ella couldn't be ill now. She didn't have an understudy and that meant the show would be cancelled!

Miss Petticoat clapped her hands and everyone settled down as she started to read. *"Dear Miss Petticoat, I'm sorry I can't do the show. Please don't cancel it. I know I don't have an understudy, but Ruby has been practicing with me and she knows my steps better than I do. Please ask her to dance."*

Miss Petticoat lowered her glasses and peered at Ruby. "Is this true, Ruby?" she asked. Ruby blushed as her classmates all turned to look at her. Shyly, she nodded.

Miss Petticoat went over to the CD player and selected the track Ella was going to dance to. "Will you show me, please?" she said.

Ruby felt her cheeks flush bright red. She hated being the centre of attention, but as she looked at the hopeful faces of her classmates, she knew what she had to do. She stepped shyly into the middle of the dance floor and stood with her arms raised high and her toes pointed. As the music played, she forgot she was being watched. She imagined she was back in Ella's living room and let the music carry her.

Ruby whirled and danced her way through the steps and, as the closing bars of the music played, swept down low and held her final pose.

Miss Petticoat clasped her hands together and cried, "Bravo, Ruby! You were magnificent! Thanks to you, the show will go on!" Ruby smiled shyly, as the rest of the class cheered. Usually she hated being the centre of attention, but for once, she didn't mind. She had to admit she'd actually quite enjoyed dancing, once she got over her nerves.

After class, Ruby hurried home to call Ella. "Sorry I dropped you in it like that, Ruby. Do you think you can do it?" croaked Ella, hoarsely.
"You sound so poorly," said Ruby, sympathetically. "Miss Petticoat made me dance and it was actually okay. So the show is still on."
"Thank you," whispered Ella, sounding very relieved. "I was scared they'd cancel it. I wish I could come and see you dance," she coughed.

Before Ruby knew it, it was the night of the show. As she sat nervously in the dressing room, fluffing her tutu, she was gripped by panic. Ruby's legs shook and her mouth felt dry as she worried that she might fall over or forget her steps. *Oh, Ella, why did you have to be ill?* she thought, feeling sick as she heard the orchestra start to tune up.

Just then, Miss Petticoat came in with some flowers and a note from Ella. Ruby smiled as she read the card, "*Dear Ruby, you know the dance better than I do. It's your chance to shine, so, have fun and make sure you come and tell me all about it. Love Ella.*"

Moments later, Ruby stood on the stage. The sudden glare of a single spotlight briefly dazzled her, but Ruby didn't falter. She began to dance and with every step her confidence grew. Soon, she was twirling and leaping across the stage, looking every bit the star of the show.

Before Ruby knew it, the music had finished and the audience were applauding, loudly. Ruby curtsied and waved at the crowd, who were all on their feet, clapping. She'd done it!

From then on, shy little Ruby, the girl who stood at the back, was no more. Instead, she danced happily at the front, where she belonged, and she loved every minute. Saving the show was the best thing that she had ever done!

101

Clumsy Clara

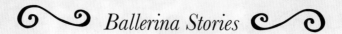

I t was the first day of the holidays and Josie was really excited. Her best friend, Clara, was coming to stay for the whole holiday. Josie was just putting her hair into bunches, when the doorbell rang. She bounded down the stairs, two at a time and smiled as her mum opened the door to Clara and her mum, Ashley.

Clara rushed into the house and hugged Josie. "I'm so excited!" she squealed. "I can't believe we've got two whole weeks together!" The girls ran, excitedly, into the garden. "We'll bring out some drinks," said Mum and she went into the kitchen with Ashley.

Outside, they all sipped glasses of lemonade. Josie's mum said, "I hear you're doing ballet, Clara. It's a shame my ballet school's shut over the holidays, otherwise you could have gone to one of the lessons," she said. "Perhaps you could do a little ballet show for us here? You could perform it for your mum when she comes to collect you?"

Josie thought this was a wonderful idea. She squeezed her friend's hand and said, "Yes, it'll be fun!" However, Clara didn't look very enthusiastic. Although she nodded in agreement, Josie could see tears in her eyes.

Later, when they were sitting on the wall, Josie said. "What's the matter?" Clara sighed, sadly. "I can't dance, Josie, I'm too clumsy." she said. Josie thought about Clara's words. Surely she could help her?

The next morning, Josie woke early and crept downstairs. She quietly opened the hall cupboard and ran her fingers along a row of hooks until she found a set of keys labelled, *'Dance School, Spare key.'* She slipped the keys into her pocket and quietly made her way back upstairs.

When Josie opened her bedroom door, Clara was sitting up in bed, rubbing her eyes, sleepily. Josie picked up Clara's clothes and handed them to her. "Come on sleepy-head, we've got work to do."

Clara looked puzzled. "However, Josie, it's the holidays," she groaned. "What's so important that we have to get up so early?" complained Clara.
"We're going to Mum's ballet studio and I'm going to teach you to dance!" replied Josie. "By the time your mum comes to pick you up, you'll be dancing like a pro!"

Soon, the girls were standing in the empty dance studio. Clara looked nervous. "This is so pointless," she muttered. "I'm just not cut out for ballet."

Josie smiled, kindly, and said, "Nonsense. Anyone can dance. You just need to believe in yourself and practice." She pressed a button and classical music filled the room. "Just follow my lead and we'll take the first position," she said.

Clara opened her mouth to protest, but Josie was so confident and sure that she could help her that Clara felt she had to try. Sighing, she brought her heels together and turned her feet out. Quietly and patiently, Josie took her friend through the five basic positions. When Clara wobbled, or got a step wrong, Josie patiently told her to try again.

For the rest of the holidays, Josie and Clara practised every day. Clara found that she wasn't as clumsy and, with Josie's kind words and patience, she got better at ballet.

A few days before Clara's mum was due to collect her, Josie said, "Right, I think you're ready to learn the routine we'll do for your mum." To her surprise, Clara nodded. "I'd like that," she said, quietly. "Thank you for helping me, Josie."

Josie smiled, happily, as she took Clara through the steps for the dance she'd come up with. She felt glad she had helped her cousin. As she watched her move confidently across the dance floor, she could see that Clara had grown to love ballet.

Someone else could see it, too. Josie's mum had popped in and, hearing a noise, had crept quietly up to the dance studio and peered nervously through the glass panel in the door. She blinked in surprise when she saw Josie, confidently teaching Clara.

As their lesson came to an end, Josie said, "See? Dancing for our mums will be fine, Clara. You just needed a little helping hand and to believe in yourself," she smiled, hugging her.

With that, Josie and Clara started to pack their things up. Meanwhile, Josie's mum tiptoed quietly away. She could see the girls had worked hard and didn't want to spoil the surprise.

The next day, Clara's mum, Ashley, arrived in her little red car, hooting loudly as she swung into the driveway. Clara rushed outside and hugged her, saying, "I've had the best time with Josie and I can't wait to show you my dance!"

Clara pulled her arm and said, "Come on, let's go straight into the garden. Everything's ready." Ashley gasped when she saw the garden. Pretty ribbons decorated the trees and Josie had hung a big sheet up as their backdrop.

Josie's mum hugged Ashley and said, "Come and take your seat for the show." Josie nodded and her mum pressed a button, so music filled the air. Clara and Josie leaped gracefully across the garden, their arms outstretched and their heads held high. "I had no idea they were so good," whispered Ashley, as she watched them dancing confidently together.

"Well, they have put in a lot of hard work," said Josie's mum. Both mums were really proud of their daughters. They both burst into applause at the end of the dance. "Bravo!" called Josie's mum as the girls hugged. They had done it! Josie felt so proud of Clara. She had danced brilliantly. "See? You can dance," she whispered in Clara's ear.

Later, as Josie watched Clara get into the car, she smiled. Her friend had blossomed into a confident ballerina and Josie couldn't have been more proud.

The Ordinary Tutu

Ava arrived at ballet class and tied her hair up in a neat bun. Then, she chatted to her best friends, Martha and Priya. They were all eagerly anticipating Miss Spin's arrival with the costumes for their ballet show.

Suddenly, the doors to the studio clattered open and all eyes were on Miss Spin, who was pushing a rail filled with different-colored outfits. "Now, line up girls, and I'll call out your names," she said, as she cast her eye down a list on her clipboard. Ava hoped her name would be called first, but it wasn't. She watched anxiously as, one by one, the costumes disappeared from the rail.

Martha skipped back, happily, with a beautiful, gold leotard and matching tutu. Then Priya's name was called and she came back with a lovely, green dress. Miss Spin looked up and clapped her hands. "Right, Ava, it's your turn!" she cried, passing her a beautiful, pink leotard with glittering sequins and the fluffiest tutu Ava had ever seen.

As Ava slipped it over her head, her classmates gasped, enviously. Ava felt like a prima ballerina, as she tried a pirouette in her beautiful costume.
"Ava, you look amazing," said Martha, and Priya nodded in agreement. Ava grinned. She was glad she'd had to wait, as Miss Spin had certainly saved the best until last.

111

The next night was the dress rehearsal. Ava eagerly rushed into the studio and slipped into her costume. She waved at Priya and Martha, who were sitting nearby. Priya smiled and said, "You look great, Ava. Your outfit is so lovely."

Smiling, happily, Ava twirled around. "I wish I could keep it forever," she sighed. Ava span and span, round and round, going faster and faster, until she was seeing stars.

"Be careful!" cried Martha, as Ava started to wobble, dizzily. She stumbled and fell hard against the door, catching her lovely tutu on the handle. A loud ripping noise made her gasp.

Ava followed Priya and Martha's horrified gazes and gasped in dismay when she saw the damage. Her tutu, which had once been so fluffy and beautiful, now hung limply with a huge, jagged tear down one side.

Martha looked at the tattered, torn edges of the tutu and said, doubtfully, "My mum might be able to sew it for you."
However, Ava shook her head. She knew the tutu was beyond repair. Huge tears began to roll down her cheeks. "How am I going to tell Miss Spin?" she cried, in despair.

"Tell me what?" said Miss Spin, as she bounced into class. Ava couldn't answer. She was crying so hard that she couldn't catch her breath. Seeing the rip in the now tattered tutu, Miss Spin frowned and said, crossly, "Whatever were you doing?"

In between sobs, Ava blurted out the whole, sorry tale. Miss Spin listened, then seeing how upset Ava was, said gently, "Well, it sounds like it was an accident. I'll have to see what we can find for you in the costume cupboard. However, it won't be a patch on this one," she warned.

Sure enough, when Miss Spin came back, Ava saw, to her horror, that she was clutching a white tutu. It had no sparkles and wasn't half as lovely as her pink one.

"It's a little plain, I'm afraid, but once you're on stage, it'll look fine," said Miss Spin, as she handed Ava the tutu.

Reluctantly, Ava slipped it on. She couldn't really complain, as it was her fault that the other tutu had ripped. Even so, she was hurt when a couple of her classmates sniggered and pointed. It wasn't surprising, really. Next to the sparkles on her pink leotard, the tutu looked so ordinary.

Seeing her gloomy face, Miss Spin whispered, "Ava, it's not about what you're wearing. Dancing comes from the heart. If you feel like a prima ballerina, you will dance like one, no matter how glittery your tutu is."

That afternoon, when Ava got home and saw her mum, she burst into tears. "I was showing off," she sobbed. "Now I have ruined the beautiful tutu."

She told her mum all about the plain, replacement tutu and what Miss Spin had said. Ava's mum made her a special treat and gave her an extra, special hug. "What Miss Spin says is true," she said, softly. "You are a good dancer and you will shine, no matter what you wear."

However, all evening, Ava thought about her ripped tutu. "I would have looked so lovely in it," she whispered to herself. "Now, no one will even notice me in this horrid, plain one."

Soon, it was time for bed. "Come on," said Mum. "Put on your pyjamas and snuggle down." Ava put on her best pyjamas. She opened her favorite ballet stories book and looked at the pages. However, they just made Ava think of the plain tutu. She imagined herself all alone on the stage, under a big spotlight. The audience were laughing at her. Even Ava's friends were laughing at her. Worst of all, Miss Spin was laughing at her.

Ava shook the thought out of her head and tried to go to sleep. Outside, the moon shone brightly and the stars twinkled. "I wish I could shine like they do," said Ava, as she finally drifted off to sleep.

The next evening, Ava was the last to arrive. She wasn't excited about the show now she didn't have her pink tutu. Holding up the ordinary, plain tutu, she sighed heavily and pulled it on. She could hardly bear to look at Martha and Priya in their colorful costumes.

Sadly, Ava took her place on stage. The music started and Ava couldn't help but feel a pang of enthusiasm. She shook all worries about the ordinary tutu from her mind. As the bright, white spotlights flicked on, she started to move. Ava's heart soared with the music, as she tiptoed across the stage. As she danced, Ava caught Martha's eye and saw her friend was staring at her tutu. Ava glanced down and her tummy fluttered.

The white tutu was sparkling and glittering under the bright lights. It was the most beautiful thing Ava had ever seen. Ava felt like a proper ballerina, as she twirled and leaped.

Afterwards, backstage, Ava cried, "Look! Miss Spin. My tutu isn't ordinary at all, it's really beautiful!" However, as she lifted the white netting, she was dismayed to see it was quite ordinary again. Miss Spin said, "See? Even the most ordinary of costumes sparkle when you dance from the heart." As she turned away, Ava could have sworn that her teacher winked.

From then on, Ava didn't mind what she wore to dance. However, she often thought about the ordinary tutu and wondered if it had been magic, or just a trick of the stage lights. One thing was for sure, though. Ava would always dance from the heart, whatever she wore.

Lisa in the Limelight

It was Wednesday evening and, as usual, that meant ballet class for Jess and her twin sister, Lisa. As the girls made their way down the street, birds chirruped and a gentle breeze blew cherry blossom across the pavements. Jess was chattering away to Lisa and, as always, Lisa was listening quietly to her outgoing sister, who was far more confident than she had ever been.

"So, Lisa, why don't you come and dance at the front with me and my friends?" said Jess. "We have such a giggle together. I don't see why you always want to hide away on your own at the back of the class?"

Lisa sighed. They had this conversation every week and Lisa always gave her sister the same response. "Oh, Jess. It's nothing personal," she said. "I just hate being in the limelight. I'd rather be at the back, where I can quietly learn the steps without looking daft if I make a mistake."

Jess smiled, sympathetically. "No one would laugh at you Lisa. After all, we're all learning." Suddenly, Jess checked her watch and said, "We'd better hurry or we'll be late and Miss Ivory said we should arrive early, to practice for Miss Jolley's visit."

Lisa in the Limelight

Dance Classes held weekly

The girls hurried to the studio. Inside, Jess took her place in the middle of the front row, next to her friends. Meanwhile, Lisa slipped to the back and stood on her own. As they warmed up, they waited patiently for their teacher, Miss Ivory. It was an important day, as Miss Jolley was visiting from the City Ballet Academy and all the girls had spent weeks practising the dance they were going to perform.

No one was surprised, however, that Miss Ivory was late. She was a lovely teacher, but she was never on time. Even so, the girls were very fond of her and Lisa was sure that at any minute she would burst through the doors, hair flying wildly, as she made some excuse about losing track of the time.

Just then, Jess's phone rang. Everyone watched as she pulled a face and nodded. Then, she turned to them and said, "Miss Ivory's lost her car keys. She said we'll have to continue practice without her. Does anyone know all the steps yet?"

The girls all looked at each other and shrugged. It seemed like no one knew all of the steps in the dance. "What are we going to do!" cried Jess, panicking. "I know the steps," said a quiet voice from the back of the room.

Lisa's legs were shaking as she walked to the front and stood in front of her classmates. They all stared at her in shock. No one could remember hearing Lisa speak in class before. She was usually so quiet and shy.

Jess hugged her sister. "You're a lifesaver, Lisa!" she cried. Lisa smiled and said, "Come on, Jess. We need to get on if we're going to learn these steps before Miss Jolley arrives. Now, take your places everyone. Follow my lead," she commanded.

Jess watched in amazement as Lisa patiently took everyone through the dance, gently helping those who were struggling. Lisa seemed different somehow. She looked confident and assured and Jess couldn't believe that her quiet, shy sister was at the front of the class, teaching!

The class followed Lisa's lead and went through the routine again and again. Lisa felt her confidence soaring as she watched her classmates eagerly following her. She'd been so scared at first, but now she was at the front, she found she was enjoying herself.

Lisa walked around the room, watching her classmates, closely. Occasionally, she stopped and whispered instructions as she gently helped one of the girls adjust their position. After a while, she nodded with satisfaction and flicked the music off. Smiling happily, Lisa turned to face the class and said, "Well done. We're ready for Miss Jolley. I hope she'll be impressed."

"I certainly am," said a voice from the side of the room. "That was a super rehearsal." Everyone turned to see who had come in and gasped when they saw Miss Jolley standing at the door with Miss Ivory, who was red-faced and flustered. "Thank you, Lisa, for stepping in like that. I mislaid my keys," she stuttered.

"Never mind," said Miss Jolley. "In a way, I'm glad you did. It's allowed one of your pupils to shine and I think she has the makings of a marvellous ballet teacher."

Lisa blushed and looked down at her ballet shoes. She shuffled about self-consciously as Miss Jolley continued to heap praise on her. Glancing up, Lisa saw Jess, smiling happily at her. Her sister gave her a thumbs up, which made Lisa blush again.

Later, Jess nudged Lisa. "See? Being in the limelight's not so bad, is it? You saved the day." Lisa smiled and said, "Okay, sis, you win. I'll stand at the front next week."

Miss Ivory hurried over and breathlessly thanked Lisa. "I'm so grateful. You're a real credit," she babbled. "In fact, Miss Jolley has offered you a place at the City Ballet Academy."

Lisa gasped. She couldn't believe it. "That's amazing!" cried Jess, scooping her sister into a huge hug. Miss Ivory, however, wasn't listening. She was rummaging through her enormous handbag. "Now, where did I put the studio keys?" she muttered.

Lisa smiled. She was glad Miss Ivory was disorganised. After all, it was thanks to her lost keys that Lisa had stepped into the limelight. Now, she would never hide in the shadows again.

May the Best Team Win

It was the annual ballet competition at the Festival Hall. Alice and her friend, Emily, put on their pink leotards in the dressing room. "I can't believe we're dancing here," said Alice to Emily. Suddenly, she felt very nervous.

Alice was worried when she saw that they were sharing the dressing room with Miss Snooty's ballet school. They had a reputation for being very unfriendly. A blonde-haired girl was scouling at them, already. "I don't think much of the competition this year, girls, do you?" sneered the girl.

Alice frowned and opened her mouth to say something back, but was interrupted by Miss Sugar, who had been talking to Miss Snooty. "Let's wish everyone good luck," she said, kindly. "May the best team win."

Miss Snooty just gave a tight smile, then turned to speak to her class. "Now as you know, girls, you'll be marked on your moves, your costumes and the music. I want you to do everything you can to make sure we win that trophy."

Suddenly, Emily gasped. "My tutu's missing!" she cried, bursting into tears as she rummaged through her ballet bag. "So's mine!" said a voice. "Mine, too," said another. Then, Alice realised hers had gone, as well.

As her friends searched for their tutus, Alice suddenly noticed that the Snooty girls were staring at them. Alice felt her cheeks flush with anger as she stamped over to them and said, "Come on then, where are they? I know you took our tutus."

The blond girl looked innocent and said, "What tutus? I don't know what you're talking about. It's a shame, though. You'll look awfully silly dancing without them. It looks like the trophy is ours again, girls!"

"Don't bet on it," snapped Emily, coming over to Alice. "You haven't seen us dance yet." The blond girl just laughed. "Snooty School always wins and, like Miss Snooty said, we'll do anything to get first place," she added, winking at Alice.

Alice's eyes flashed with anger. "Well, maybe this time you've met your match!" she said as she and Emily turned smartly on their heels and made their way back to the rest of the class. Emily was determined not to be beaten by a bunch of cheats.

"They're cheating," muttered Alice, as she seethed about the missing tutus. She was so sure that the blond girl had taken them. It was such a mean thing to do, but now she was determined to win the competition fairly.

"We'll dance, tutus or no tutus," said Miss Sugar, firmly as she handed a tissue to one of the younger girls, who was still crying. "Now, let's go outside for some fresh air."

Miss Sugar led the girls to a patch of grass, next to the hall and they sat down in the shade, as she handed out some drinks. "Now, girls, I don't know what happened to your tutus, but I want you to go out there and do your best. I want you to rise above the daft talk from the Snooty girls. They're just trying to scare you. Remember, the winners will be judged by their performance, nothing else, so don't let them get to you."

Alice smiled. As usual, Miss Sugar always knew just the right thing to say and now she felt sure that the competition would go well, with or without their tutus. "Don't worry, Miss Sugar, we won't let you down," she said, as they made their way inside.

An hour later, the girls were ready to perform. Alice checked the ribbons on her slippers for what seemed like the hundredth time. Nerves fluttered in her tummy and her legs felt like jelly, as they waited to be called on stage. "I'm so nervous," whispered Emily. Alice smiled and said, "Forget your nerves, let's just concentrate on winning that trophy."

"You won't be winning anything if I can't find the sheet music!" cried Miss Sugar, as she searched through her papers again. "I know it was here. I checked just before we went outside." Alice and Emily exchanged looks. Had the girls from Snooty School taken the music, too?

"Oh, no, they're going to beat us!" cried Alice. Miss Sugar looked thoughtful. "No, they aren't," she said. "As it happens, I chose my favorite piece of music for this performance. I know it off by heart. I don't need the music sheets to play it!"

Just then, Snooty School came off stage. They were sure that their opponents would not be able to dance without their music. However, they were in for a shock.

The class took their positions on stage and Miss Sugar began to play. Everyone danced their hearts out. None more so than Alice. She forgot all about the unkindness of the Snooty Girls and, as she whirled around in the glare of the lights, she felt lighter than air.

The final notes of the music died away and the applause was deafening. The judges stood and clapped as Alice and her friends proudly took their bows. "Bravo, girls," said one of the judges. "I'm pleased to announce that you are this year's winners. It was a bold move not to wear tutus, but we liked it. Well done. Here are last year's winners to present your trophy."

Alice watched with a smile of satisfaction on her face as a furious Miss Snooty reluctantly handed the trophy over to Miss Sugar.

Later, as they made their way back to the dressing room, Miss Sugar hugged Alice and said, "See? I told you that the best team would win!" and Alice couldn't have agreed more.

Goodbye, Miss Sweet

It was the end of Amy's ballet class. She had worn her new pink leotard and brown skirt to show her teacher, Miss Sweet. Amy thought Miss Sweet was the best teacher ever and wanted to impress her. "You look very nice, my dear," said Miss Sweet, then she clapped her hands and cleared her throat. "Girls, I have an announcement to make," she said, her kind, blue eyes filling with tears. "I'm retiring from teaching. I'll still own the school and pop in from time to time, but a new teacher will take your lesson next week."

The girls looked at each other in amazement. What would they do without Miss Sweet?"Please don't go!" begged Amy. "You're the best teacher we've ever had."

Miss Sweet took off her glasses and dabbed the tears from her eyes. "I'm sure the new teacher will be fine," she said, sadly.

Amy and her best friend, Hannah, said their goodbyes to Miss Sweet and walked home. "I wonder if our new teacher will be as kind as Miss Sweet?" said Amy, swinging her ballet bag, as they wandered along slowly.

"I don't think anyone could be a patch on Miss Sweet," replied Hannah. "She's so lovely and kind. Do you remember when I first started ballet and I wasn't very good? She was so patient with me."

Amy smiled as she remembered how Hannah's confidence had grown with Miss Sweet's gentle encouragement. "Well, hopefully, the new teacher will be nice," said Amy, as they reached her front gate. "We'll just have to wait until next week to find out."

137

The next week, Amy and Hannah couldn't wait to get to class. They were keen to meet their new teacher and had spent days imagining what she would be like. However, when they stepped into the dance studio, there was none of the usual bustle and chatter. Instead, their classmates were sitting quietly in a neat little row, looking very nervous.

"So, you've finally decided to join us," said a sharp voice. "You're late. That's a black mark for each of you."

Amy and Hannah turned round and found themselves face to face with a tall, bony woman. She had sharp features and a thin, mean-looking mouth. As Amy sat down, her heart sank. Could this really be their new teacher?

"I'm Miss Steel and from now on, class will be run my way. Everyone is to be on time. You will change in silence. Anyone with the wrong kit will be sent home. You will dance in silence. Rule-breakers get a black mark. Two black marks earn you a detention. Do I make myself clear?"

Amy felt really upset. "It's alright," said Hannah, trying to comfort her. "No talking!" barked Miss Steel. "That's another black mark!"

By the end of the class, almost everyone had two black marks. Miss Steel seemed to delight in keeping everyone back for extra practice and, by the time she let them go, the girls were all exhausted. "What an awful woman!" cried Amy, as soon as they were outside. "It's meant to be a ballet school, not boot camp!"

When it was time for their next class, Amy was panicking. She couldn't find her pink leotard and, as the minutes ticked by, she had no choice but to throw a white one in her bag. She didn't dare be late as well. She raced to Hannah's house and, together, they sprinted to class as fast as they could.

When they arrived, Miss Steel was waiting for them, her face flushed with anger. "You're a minute late!" she said. "That's a black mark for both of you. Now get changed!" she barked.

Shortly after, when they lined up for the kit inspection, Miss Steel eyed Amy's white leotard and tapped her on the shoulder. "You're in the wrong kit. Get changed and go home," she ordered, as Amy's lip wobbled and a tear rolled down her cheek.

Amy quickly threw her t-shirt and jeans over her ballet kit and rushed outside.
I hate ballet and I hate Miss Steel! she thought, bursting into tears. Amy wished more than anything that Miss Sweet hadn't retired.

"Whatever's the matter, Amy?" said a voice. Amy turned round and saw Miss Sweet standing nearby, frowning with concern when she saw Amy's tear-stained cheeks. Amy was so glad to see her old teacher that she ran to her and the whole story came tumbling out.

After she'd finished, Miss Sweet said, quietly, "You don't have to go home. Ballet is supposed to be fun, not an ordeal." Then, she led Amy back into the building and took her back to the studio.

Inside, the girls looked miserable as they warmed up in silence. Miss Steel moved amongst them, handing out black marks for the smallest of mistakes.

When the door opened and Miss Sweet came in, with a reassuring hand on Amy's shoulder, Miss Steel looked startled. "What's she doing here?" she demanded. "I sent her home."

"I know you did," said Miss Sweet, quietly. "But I brought her back. I've heard about your black marks and silly punishments and I don't like it one bit."
"The girls lack discipline!" shouted Miss Steel. "My punishments will help them learn."

To her surprise, Miss Sweet shook her head. "Not in my school, they won't. My girls learn by encouragement and praise. If you don't like it, Miss Steel, I suggest you find a new job."

Miss Steel's eyes flashed with anger. She scooped up her belongings and stalked out of the room. The class erupted into cheers and applause. Horrid Miss Steel was gone for good!

"Right, girls, where were you?" said Miss Sweet, her eyes twinkling. Amy hugged Hannah and the two friends leapt up and down. Their beloved Miss Sweet was back.

"But what about your retirement?" asked Amy. Miss Sweet smiled and replied, "To be honest, retirement's not for me. It's rather boring, actually. So, I'm afraid you're stuck with me for a few more years!"

The class cheered in delight as Miss Sweet began their warm up. She was back where she belonged and Amy knew that from then on, ballet would always be fun.

Flowers for Princess Prunella

At Miss Treacle's Ballet School, everyone was very excited. They had just found out that Princess Prunella would be guest of honor at the County Dance Show. The girls had squealed with joy when Miss Treacle told them. "That's not all, girls," she added. "We've been chosen for a very special job. One of you will present a bouquet to the princess."

Faye held her breath and shut her eyes. She imagined herself gliding up to the stage and smiling at Princess Prunella, as she gave her a beautiful bunch of red roses, then curtsied elegantly. How she longed to be the one who presented the bouquet.

Her daydream was interrupted by bossy Alice, who said, "I think I should do it. After all, my dad does own the school."

The girls all sighed and rolled their eyes. They were all a little sick of hearing Alice tell everyone how good she was. Alice shook her blond hair and continued. "Think about it Miss Treacle," she said. "You can't let Elsa do it. She's too clumsy. She's bound to trip. Harriet's always late and Rhea's too scruffy. It's clear I'm the best girl for the job."

Miss Treacle looked round the room. Elsa, Harriet and Rhea all looked really upset. "Don't be so unkind to your classmates, Alice. The fairest way to do it is to hold a dance-off. The best dancer will get the job," she said, firmly.

Miss Treacle clapped her hands and the girls eagerly took their positions, all keen to win the dance-off. "We'll dance the routine for the show," she said. "If I tap you on the shoulder, please sit down."

With that, the music started. All the girls danced their hearts out. Faye concentrated very hard. She was desperate to win, but felt sure that she was too quiet and shy to be noticed. She sighed as she saw Alice throwing herself around, flamboyantly. Alice had ruffled a few feathers since she started at the school. *If only she wasn't quite so brash,* thought Faye. She was sure that underneath, Alice was quite nice, really.

Miss Treacle walked around the room and started to tap people on the shoulder.

One by one, girls left the floor, until there was just Faye and Alice left. Alice tried even harder. Her moves became dramatic and showy and the girls sitting at the side started to giggle. Faye ignored the distractions around her and concentrated on dancing precisely and gracefully. Even so, she was speechless when she saw Miss Treacle approach Alice and tap her on the shoulder.

Alice blushed, furiously. She couldn't believe that she'd lost to Faye. "Miss Treacle, you're making a mistake. I'm definitely the best girl for the job!" she cried, looking very angry.

Miss Treacle held her hand up. "I've made my decision, Alice. Besides, I want someone who can present the bouquet quietly," she said. Alice began to look upset and stomped off to a corner to be on her own.

Faye's heart soared, as Miss Treacle said, "Congratulations, Faye. Can you stay behind after class so we can run through what to do?"

Faye smiled, happily. She couldn't believe that tomorrow evening she'd be meeting a real princess. She was about to reply to Miss Treacle, when she noticed out of the corner of her eye that Alice was sitting with her head on her knees, sobbing. Faye hated seeing anyone upset, so she excused herself and sat down, next to Alice.

"Have you come to laugh at me?" said Alice, bitterly, as tears rolled down her cheeks. "No, of course not," replied Faye. "I came over because you're upset."
"I always mess everything up," sniffed Alice, as she wiped her eyes, crossly. "I haven't got any friends and now I won't get to meet Princess Prunella, either."

Faye put her hand gently on Alice's arm. "You just need to tone things down a bit. You come on a bit strong, sometimes," she said, kindly.
"I try to impress people so they'll like me," said Alice, sadly. "Because Dad owns the school, I feel like I have to be the best at everything."

Faye hugged her and said, "You just have to be yourself. Don't worry, I think I know how I can make things better." With that, she hurried off to see Miss Treacle.

Alice watched curiously as she saw Faye speaking quietly and urgently to their teacher. Miss Treacle frowned as Faye talked, then called Alice over. "Alice, Faye wants you to present the bouquet with her," said Miss Treacle. Alice felt a little ashamed. She'd behaved terribly and Faye had still been kind to her. "I won't let you down," she promised, quietly.

The next evening, the local theater hummed as, one by one, the dance schools performed to the packed audience. Princess Prunella sat and watched the dancing, with a smile on her face. She had loved ballet when she was a child and the evening was bringing back happy memories.

Miss Treacle's class danced beautifully. Everyone whooped and cheered as they took their bows. Faye was feeling nervous because she knew her big moment had arrived. She took her place in the wings, next to Alice. Faye noticed that Alice was holding the bouquet and her heart sank. Miss Treacle had wanted Faye to present the flowers, but it looked like Alice had other ideas. *She hasn't changed at all*, thought Faye.

It looked like Alice would be presenting the flowers after all. As they waited for their cue, Alice hesitated and handed the bouquet to Faye. "You give it to the Princess," she whispered. Faye smiled. "Thanks, Alice. That's really kind of you," she said. "No, you're the kind one," replied Alice. "You've made me see that shouting doesn't get you what you want. I'd like it if we could be friends," she added, shyly.

Faye was delighted. "I'd like that, too," she said, as together they stepped out into the spotlight. The friends curtsied, elegantly, before the Princess and Faye handed her the flowers. Faye smiled, happily, as they shook Princess Prunella's hand. She was glad she'd given Alice a chance. Now, everyone was happy!

Boys Don't Dance

It was a very rainy day and Emily was late for class. She grabbed her raincoat and her umbrella and dashed outside. "Where are you going?" said her little brother, Alex. "To my ballet class," replied Emily, ruffling his hair. "I'll be back soon."

"Can I come, too?" asked Alex, pulling on his shiny, red wellingtons and his rain jacket. "No, Alex, you need to stay here, with Mummy," said Emily, firmly. With that, she dashed off towards the ballet school. Cars swished past with their headlights on in the afternoon gloom, splashing water onto the pavements.

Soon, the welcoming lights of the ballet school appeared ahead. Emily skipped up the steps and through the doors. She turned round and gasped when she saw Alex behind her, his hair plastered to his head and rain dripping off his coat. "Alex!" she cried. "I told you to stay at home!"

Alex's bottom lip began to wobble. "I only wanted to see you dance," he said. Sighing, Emily dried his rain-soaked face, then went to find Miss Slipper, her teacher. "Don't worry," said Miss Slipper, kindly. "Alex can stay and watch. I'll call your mum to say he's safe," she added, patting Emily on the arm.

153

At first, while Emily and her friends warmed up, Alex sat on a little bench at the back, swinging his feet in time to the music. He watched with interest as Miss Slipper took her place at the front of the class and clapped her hands. "First position, please," she called.

The girls all stood, hands in front of hips, with their heels together and their toes turned out. Emily could hear a couple of her friends giggling and whispering. She glanced back to Alex and blushed when she saw he was on his feet, trying to copy their pose. "Boys don't dance, Alex!" she hissed. "Go and sit down!"

However, Alex didn't listen. Every time Miss Slipper clapped her hands and the class took another position, Alex did, too! He was wobbly and uncertain, but he tried his very best.

Miss Slipper clapped her hands once again and the class took their positions to practice the dance they had been learning. Emily's ears burned bright red as she heard her friends whispering and tittering again. She turned round and looked for Alex. She cringed when she saw he was standing next to one of the other girls, copying her leg lift. The girl grinned and said, "Awww, that's so sweet!"

Emily didn't think it was sweet. She felt cross. Alex was ruining her ballet class and he shouldn't even be there. *Boys are supposed to play football, not dance,* she thought crossly, as she left her place and led Alex back to the bench.

Blushing furiously, she hissed, "Alex, please sit down. Boys don't dance."

Every time Emily looked, Alex was dancing, copying the steps as best he could. She'd given up taking him back to the bench, as he just get straight back up again, dancing and twirling. Emily smiled awkwardly at Miss Sugar and mouthed, "Sorry!" However, her teacher seemed quite amused by Alex's antics. Her eyes twinkled as she watched him spin and jump his way through the rest of the lesson.

Emily was beginning to think the class would never end when Miss Slipper clapped her hands and brought her humiliation to an end. Emily marched over to Alex. "I told you to sit on the bench, Alex!" she said, crossly. "You've ruined my class. I've told you, boys don't dance."

"Actually, boys do dance, Emily," said Miss Slipper. "We don't have many in the school, but I have taught a few in my time. I think Alex dances very well – just like his big sister," she added. "Would you like to come next week?" she asked Alex as he gave a huge, happy smile. "Oooh! Yes please!" he cried, jumping up and down with excitement.

Emily frowned. The thought of another class like today's made her heart sink. "Oh, don't worry, Emily, Alex is too young for this class," said Miss Slipper. "He'll join our class for under fives," she explained, as Emily felt a pang of relief. She had to admit, Alex had been quite good at ballet and he certainly seemed to enjoy it.

157

Next week, Emily sat on the bench at the back of the class and watched, proudly, as her brother lined up with the other children. She was surprised to see that there was another boy in the class, too. They stood next to each other and watched Miss Slipper as she showed them the first position.

Alex was concentrating really hard and Emily beamed, as she saw his feet were positioned perfectly. Maybe she'd been too hasty when she thought ballet was just for girls. Alex seemed to be a natural dancer. She grinned to herself, as she imagined them dancing together when they were older. *Perhaps it isn't so bad having a brother who dances,* she thought.

158

The music started and the under fives teacher, Miss Frill, stood in front of the class. "Come along now, children," she said. "Follow me. One and two and three and four." Emily watched, as Alex copied all the moves perfectly.

Miss Frill told the children to run round in a circle and wave their arms as if they were flying. Alex pointed his toes, held his arms up beautifully and glided round the room. Emily was very impressed. Miss Frill was impressed, too. "Well done, Alex," she said. "Considering that you are new to ballet, you have done really well."
The other children smiled at Alex. He was fitting in already and he loved the twinkle toes class.

At the end of the class, Alex skipped over to Emily, his eyes shining with excitement. "That was brilliant, Emily. Can I come again, please?" he begged, hopping from foot to foot.

Emily grinned. "We'll ask Mum, but I'm sure she'll say yes," she replied, giving her brother a hug. "Well done, Alex, you worked really hard today."
Miss Slipper patted Alex on the back and said, "That was great, Alex." Turning to Emily, she added, "See, Emily? Boys do dance and some of them do it very well indeed!"

Emily had to agree that Miss Slipper was right, Alex was very good. As they made their way home, hand in hand, Emily felt very proud of her little brother. She smiled at him and said, "Come on, my little ballet star, never again will I say that boys don't dance!"